Long Ago Yesterday

Stories and pictures by
Anne Rockwell

Greenwillow Books, New York

CONTENTS

THE SNOWY GIRL

Not so long ago a little girl was sleeping in her warm bed while snowflakes began to fall. When the little girl woke up, the ground was covered with snow. Everything was white and bumpy-shaped and very quiet.

The little girl put on her woolly hat, her red snowsuit, her scarf, her boots, and her warm mittens. "Look at me!" she said to her mother and father. "Now I'm a snowy girl!"

She went outside and made deep footprints in the bright, white snow. She helped shovel a path to the door. She lay down in the snow and made a snow angel.

Her mother and father helped her build a snowman. The snowman watched the snowy girl go for a ride on her sled. He watched her throw snowballs to her mother and father.

He watched the orange snowplow clear a path down the street, making loud scraping noises as it did.

After a while the little girl's mother and father wanted to go inside and get warm, but the snowy girl said, "No, I can't go inside. I am a snowy girl!" So they stayed outside with her.

Soon the snowy girl's snowsuit was not red any more. It was white with all the snow that covered it. Her scarf was covered with snow, and so were her hat and mittens.

Her mother went inside. Soon she called, "Cocoa's ready!"

By now even the snowy girl felt cold. She said, "See you later, snowman," and she and her father went inside.

She took off her snowsuit, and her mother put it in the dryer with her hat, her scarf, and her mittens. Then the snowy girl sat down with her mother and father at the kitchen table and drank hot cocoa with white marshmallows melting on top, and they all got nice and warm.

A HONEY BEAR

Not so long ago there was a little boy who decided he wanted to be a honey bear. "Umph! Umph!" he grunted. "I want honey!" So his mother put a spoonful of honey on his cereal.

All morning he walked on all fours like a honey bear and talked in happy grunts.

When his father came home for supper, he picked up his little boy and said, "How's my big boy today?"

The little boy said, "I'm not a boy. I'm a honey bear! Umph! Umph! I want honey!" His father gave him a saucer of honey, and the honey bear grunted "Umph! Umph!" and ate it all up.

After supper his mother and father took him upstairs. When his mother took his nice warm pajamas out of the drawer, he grunted, "Umph! Umph! No pajamas! I'm a honey bear with warm fur, and honey bears don't wear pajamas!"

"That's true, they don't," said his mother. So he didn't wear any.

When his father found a book called *Tommy the Airplane Pilot* and started to read it, the honey bear grunted, "Umph! Umph! Bears only like books about honey."

His father found a book about a bumblebee. "How's this?" he asked. "Bees make honey."

The honey bear grunted, "Umph! Umph! Read me that story." Then it was time to tuck him in and turn out the light. "Good-night, Honey Bear," said his mother and father.

But as soon as they turned out the light, the honey bear began to cry. "What's the matter?" asked his mother.

"Don't say 'Good-night, Honey Bear.' I'm not a honey bear! I'm your very own little boy, and I'm cold. I want my pajamas!"

"Of course you're our very own little boy," said his father, and gave him a big bear hug.

The little boy put on his pajamas. He kissed his mother and father good-night, and they turned out the light and tiptoed out of their little boy's room.

A LONG, LONG JOURNEY

Not so long ago there was a little girl who was going on a journey to someplace far away.

The little girl's mother strapped her into her car seat. Then she and the little girl's father got in the car and fastened their seat belts, too. The little girl's father put the key in the ignition. But as soon as he did, he said, "I'll have to get gas!"

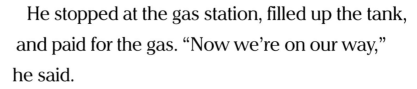

He stopped at the gas station, filled up the tank, and paid for the gas. "Now we're on our way," he said.

He drove and drove until the little girl got tired of watching noisy cars and trucks zoom by. "Are we there yet?" she asked.

"Not yet," said her mother.

They stopped in a parking lot. "Are we there?" asked the little girl, but they weren't. They were only stopping for lunch and to go to the bathroom.

After lunch they got in the car and drove and drove until they

turned off the big highway onto a side road.

After a while they came to a town. The little girl's mother said, "I don't remember this town."

"Neither do I," said the little girl's father. He stopped and looked at a map. "I was supposed to turn back there," he said.

He drove back and turned where he should have. Soon the road went past a farm with cows and a big white barn. It went past a field full of corn and came to a deep, dark woods. In those deep, dark woods the car turned onto a dirt road. It went bumpety-bump down the dirt road.

Soon they came to a big blue lake where a bullfrog jumped into the water with a loud "kerplunk." The little girl's father drove the car right up to a log cabin by the lake.

"Are we there yet?" asked the little girl.

"Yes—at last!" said her mother and father.

They unpacked the car, went into the cabin, put on their bathing suits, and—just like the bullfrog—they all went swimming in the big blue lake.

THE SCARED PUPPY

Not so long ago there was a little boy who had a puppy. He loved it very much. He would toss a rubber bone for his puppy to fetch. The puppy was very good at fetching.

He gave his puppy dog biscuits for a treat, and the puppy just loved those dog biscuits.

One day a big black cloud covered the sky above the little boy's house. Thunder rumbled and lightning flashed.

The little boy wasn't afraid, but his puppy was. It had never heard thunder, never seen lightning. It began to whimper and cry. It was so scared that it hid under the biggest chair in the living room.

"Don't be scared," the little boy said. "It's only thunder. Come out and play." But his puppy wouldn't. It just shook and trembled and whimpered under the chair.

The little boy got a dog biscuit. "Here's a dog biscuit," he said. But the puppy wouldn't come out from under the chair.

The little boy went and got the rubber bone. But his puppy wouldn't fetch it. Then the little boy rolled a ball with a jingly bell

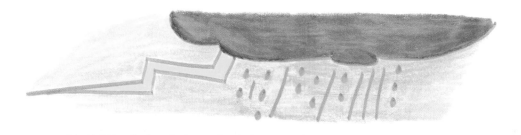

in it across the living room floor. But instead of the happy sound of a jingly bell, the air was filled with the noise of thunder. The puppy wouldn't come out to play.

The little boy went upstairs and got a blanket that had been his when he was a baby. He reached under the chair and lifted out his trembling puppy. He wrapped it in the blanket. "Don't be scared," he said. "It's only thunder and lightning making all that noise."

He cuddled his puppy close while thunder rumbled and lightning flashed.

The little boy and his puppy sat by the window and watched the rain come down. But after a while it stopped, and a rainbow appeared in the sky. The sun shone. The thunder and lightning were gone, and the puppy wasn't scared any more.

The little boy put on his boots, and he and his puppy went outside to play in the splashy, squishy-squashy, muddy yard.

BUBBLE GUM

Not so long ago there was a little girl whose big sister was always chewing bubble gum, always blowing beautiful big, pink bubbles. The little girl loved the smell of that bubble gum. She loved to watch those shiny pink bubbles grow bigger and bigger.

One day she asked her mother and father if she could have some bubble gum, but they said not yet. She was too little. She asked her teacher at day care if she could have some bubble gum, but her teacher didn't have any. So the little girl had no bubble gum, but she kept wishing she did.

One day her big sister gave her some. She showed the little girl how to chew the wad of pink bubble gum until it was just right. She showed her how to blow a bubble.

At first the little girl couldn't blow a bubble, but she practiced and practiced— and then she could. She blew and blew,

and her bubble grew bigger and bigger. It grew so big it went P O P! It popped all over the little girl's face, her nose, her cheeks, and even her hair.

Her sister tried to rub the bubble gum off. She got most of it off the little girl's nose and cheeks—but she couldn't get it out of her hair. The little girl's mother couldn't get it out of her hair. Neither could her father.

Finally her father got a pair of scissors and cut off the hair that had pink bubble gum stuck on it. Then he had to cut the rest of the little girl's hair to even it out.

The next time that little girl chewed bubble gum, she was bigger. Her bubble didn't pop until she wanted it to. Then she sucked the bubble back into her mouth, just as her sister had taught her, and blew an even bigger bubble.

"Wow! That sure is some bubble," the little girl's big sister said, and blew a great big bubble of her own.

A MIDDLE-SIZED BOY

Not so long ago there was a little boy who wished he was a big boy. But no matter how much he wanted to be big, that little boy was still little. His mother said so, and his father did, too. His baby-sitter said so, and his big sister said so every single day.

The little boy's sister went to school every morning while he went to his baby-sitter's house and his mother and father went to work. She went to piano lessons on Tuesday after school and tap-dancing lessons on Saturday. She could ride a bicycle without tipping over. She had a tank of fish she took care of all by herself. And she was such a big girl that she said the little boy was too little to play with her.

One day the little boy's mother and father and big sister blew up balloons and set the table. His baby-sitter arrived with a present. His big sister,

mother, and father put presents on the table. There was a balloon and a party hat for everyone.

A cake with candles and white icing was in front of the little boy. Everyone sang, "Happy Birthday to You."

The little boy huffed and puffed and blew out all the candles.

"What a smart boy you are!" said his baby-sitter.

"That's because I'm bigger now," the little boy said. "Now I am a middle-sized boy." And he took a big bite of his birthday cake.

The next day he went to visit a school that had lots of other middle-sized boys and girls, plenty of books to look at and listen to, interesting things to work and play with, nice teachers, a playground, and cubbies for hats and coats.

He liked that school. The middle-sized boy began to go there every day. Soon he was big enough to find middle C on the piano, do a soft-shoe shuffle, and help his sister feed the fish.

"What a big boy you are!" said his sister.

And she was right. He was.

ALIENS

Not so long ago there was a little girl who loved to visit her grandmother and look at the picture of herself when she was a tiny baby. It was in a shiny silver frame. After the little girl finished looking at the picture, her grandmother always put it back on the bookshelf where it belonged.

One day the telephone rang in the kitchen. While her grandmother went to answer it, the little girl reached up to get the picture. She held it carefully, but it slipped out of her hands. The glass shattered all over the floor.

The little girl's grandmother came running. "What happened?" she cried.

The little girl didn't say anything at first, but then she whispered, "Aliens broke it. Aliens from outer space."

"The kind in that cartoon on TV?" the little girl's grandmother asked, and the little girl nodded. "Oh—those naughty aliens!"

said the little girl's grandmother. "They haven't been to visit me since your father was a small boy. I hope they didn't hurt themselves."

"They didn't," said the little girl.

As soon as the little girl's grandmother had swept up the pieces of glass, the two of them walked down the street to the camera store. "Uh-oh! What happened?" the man in the store said when he saw the frame.

"I'm afraid some aliens broke the glass," the little girl's grandmother said.

"Wow—those aliens!" the man said. "They're always up to something. You have to watch out for them."

He got his cutting tool and cut a brand-new piece of glass. He put it in the shiny silver frame, and it fit perfectly. The little girl's grandmother paid him and thanked him.

As they walked home, the little girl said, "Grandma, aliens from outer space didn't really break the glass."

"I see," said her grandmother.

"Can we still pretend they did?" asked the little girl.

"Sure we can," said her grandmother.

They walked back to the house and put the picture back where it belonged. It never fell down again.

A BIG BROWN BOX

Not so long ago there was a little boy who wanted a tricycle very badly. One day a delivery man brought a big brown box with a picture of a tricycle on it.

The little boy was very, very happy. "Can I open it?" he asked his mother.

"You'd better wait for Daddy," she said.

The little boy waited until his father came home from the supermarket. "Now can I open my big brown box?" he said.

"I think I'd better do it myself," his father said.

The little boy watched eagerly as his father opened the big brown box. But there was no tricycle inside. There were lots of things, but not one was a tricycle. The little boy began to cry. "Look what Daddy did!" he said to his mother. "He opened the box and broke my tricycle all to pieces."

"Don't worry," his father said, and took his toolbox out of the closet. "It isn't broken. I'll put it together as soon as I read the instructions."

He read the instructions, but those pieces on the floor just didn't turn into a tricycle. The little boy and his mother and father looked at all the pieces lying on the floor, and the little boy began to cry again.

"I'll ask our neighbor to help," the little boy's father said.

The neighbor read the instructions, but he couldn't make all those pieces turn into a tricycle, either.

The little boy's mother picked up one of the pieces and said, "Hey! I think this should go here!"

"You're right!" the neighbor said. "And that should go there!"

Soon there was a brand-new tricycle in the living room! It looked exactly like the picture on the big brown box.

The little boy knew just how to ride that tricycle. He rode it around the living room, through the dining room, and into the kitchen. His father helped him out the door, and the little boy rode his brand-new tricycle up and down the driveway while his mother, his father, and the neighbor all cheered.

BY THE LIGHT OF THE MOON

Not so long ago there was a little girl who had a rag doll with a happy smile, yarn hair, a calico dress, and shiny black patent leather shoes. Her name was Dolly, and wherever the little girl went, Dolly went, too.

One afternoon the little girl and Dolly went to the park with a new baby-sitter. The little girl was having such a good time that when it was time to go, she didn't want to. So finally the baby-sitter just put her in the stroller and wheeled her home.

That night at supper, after the baby-sitter had left for the day, the little girl saw that Dolly wasn't in her chair. She wasn't in the little girl's room. The little girl didn't know where she was. She was very sad, but then she remembered.

It was dark outside, and the moon was big and white and round when the little girl and her father walked down the street, past the neighbors' houses, to the stop sign on the corner. They crossed the street and came to the park.

A night watchman was standing by the park gate. He had a big ring of keys in his hand, for he was just about to lock up.

The little girl's father told him why they had come, and the three of them walked through the green and empty park until they got to the playground.

As soon as the little girl saw Dolly sitting in the sandbox, she ran over, picked her up, and gave her a hug. Dolly was smiling as though it hadn't been the least bit scary all alone in the sandbox. "Dolly is very brave," the little girl said.

"Yes—but I'm sure she's mighty glad to see you," the little girl's father said.

He thanked the night watchman for letting them into the park. The night watchman said good-night, and locked the gate. Then the little girl, her father, and Dolly walked home by the happy light of the big, round moon.

LULLABY AND GOOD-NIGHT

Not so long ago there was a little boy who was almost ready for bed.

As soon as he had brushed his teeth, he got into bed with his teddy bear, his red fire engine, his flying superhero, and Monkey-Monkey. His mother read him a story. Then she tucked him in, said good-night, and turned out the light. But as soon as she did, her little boy said, "You forgot the lullaby."

Now this mother had never sung her little boy a lullaby. But it seemed like a fine idea, and there was one that she remembered from long ago. "All right," she said, as she sat down in the chair by his bed. "But you must promise to close your eyes and go to sleep."

She began to sing, "Lullaby and good-night . . ."

"No, no—that's not it," the little boy said. "I mean this one." He began to sing.

"That's a beautiful lullaby," his mother said. "But I don't know how to sing it. I've never heard it before."

"That's because I made it up all by myself today. Listen."

The little boy sang about dinosaurs dreaming in a long-ago land, eighteen-wheelers rolling bravely through the night, kangaroos dozing beneath the stars, pirates rocking in ships on faraway seas, and bears asleep in warm, dark caves. He sang to his teddy bear, his flying superhero, his red fire engine, Monkey-Monkey, and his mother.

They were very quiet as they listened in the darkness. The sky filled with stars as the little boy sang on. His mother closed her eyes, and before you know it, she was fast asleep in the chair in her little boy's room.

The little boy put his head on his pillow and pulled the blanket up around his shoulders. He closed his eyes, still softly humming the tune of the lullaby he had made up all by himself. Soon he and his teddy bear, his flying superhero, his red fire engine, and Monkey-Monkey were all sound asleep.

For Murielle and Gordon

Colored pencils and a felt-tipped pen were used for the full-color art.
The text type is Cheltenham Book.

First Edition   10 9 8 7 6 5 4 3 2 1

Library of Congress Cataloging-in-Publication Data

Rockwell, Anne F.
Long ago yesterday / by Anne F. Rockwell.
p.   cm.
Summary: A series of stories about events in the
everyday lives of ten very young children.
ISBN 0-688-14411-X
1. Children's stories, American.   [1. Short stories.]   I. Title.
PZ7.R5943Lo   1999   [E]—dc21   98-35267   CIP   AC